HIDDEN VEIL

SIR PATRICK BIJOU

PRELUDE

Enter a World Where Things Aren't Always as They Seem - In the Dead of Night, Go on an Adventure, Seek the Truth, and Finally Look Past the Hidden Veil. *With death plaguing her dreams, Elizabeth was sure that what she possessed was a curse.*

Every night, Elizabeth Scottson would get ready to sleep by sitting on her bed, dressed in her full-length nightgown, with a good book.

As she flipped the last page of her book closed, Elizabeth would sigh satisfaction as she savoured the ending of a good book. She would glance at her phone, see it was already midnight, and wrap her cosy blanket around her before drifting off to sleep.

It was always the same routine with the same mysterious dream every night, but it would always end with a different death.

You see, Elizabeth Scottson was born with a special gift. She could see into the future while she dreamt and try as she might to change the outcome; whatever she saw in her dreams was bound to come true.

With a strange woman visiting her dreams every night, death always finding her, and brutal deaths too similar to her dreams to be a coincidence, Elizabeth must find a way to look past the veil over her eyes. Get lost in this spine-chilling thriller and work alongside Elizabeth and Detective Parker as they race against the clock to stop the woman haunting innocent women and plaguing Elizabeth's dreams.

ABOUT THE AUTHOR

Sir Patrick Bijou lives and writes from the United Kingdom and is the author of several books on finance and fiction. He is known for his extraordinary skills in settling and negotiating peace settlements and international law and is a prodigious legal and political adviser. His diverse writing ability has been influenced by many experiences, making him the success he is today.

Sir Patrick has written many books and articles about the liberation of people, highlighting the issues of those whom the literary world of creative writing has not enlightened. His expedition into content writing has made him a remarkably inspired author and professional communicator.

He has written over 40 non-fictional and fictional books spanning different genres.

Finding his Books.

To find out more about Sir Patrick, visit his website.

www.sirpatrickbijou.com
www.bijouebook.com

Elizabeth Scottson sat down on her bed in her knee- length nightgown, a horror book in her hands, her lips pressed into a tight line. Elizabeth had always loved reading. It was one of her favorite things to do.

As she flipped through the last pages, a sigh of satisfaction left her lips. At least the ending was good; she thought as she placed the book on her bedside table.

She glanced at her phone. It was past midnight.

A soft yawn escaped her lips as she put the phone on the nightstand.

She lay on her pastel pink bed. She was immediately lulled to sleep as she pulled the blanket upon herself.

Elizabeth's blonde locks whipped furiously around her face as the wind stormed forth, brandishing a fury never known to man.

Its wrath turned everything into havoc. People were flying in the air, some already lulled into an eternal slumber, their arms flailing. Loud shrieks were muffled by the loud booms of electrifying rage, flashing in the skies every second or two.

Her body was still. It didn't seem to be affected by the cold wind that hit her face. Her body felt a sense of pleasure seeing the chaotic mess.

A green aura glowed dimly around her body; a bloodshot white now surrounded her green irises. She was in no way enjoying this. She screamed, cried, and yearned to help the people around her. But her feet were glued to the ground.

All of a sudden, the world paused.

She tried to move, and surprisingly enough, her

body obeyed. The only thing that crossed her mind was to help the people around her.

As she made her way towards their direction, a piercing pain rose in her chest. It was as if someone had passed a rope through her stomach with a sharp end and was pulling it from the other side. It was pulling her back.

She tried to force herself forward, but in one swift motion, she was snatched backward into the dark woods.

Realizing that it was of no avail, she stood up and strolled her way through the woods, moving in the direction her captor wanted her to go.

She finally reached a clearance. The pull was gone.

The forest floor shimmered in the pale moonlight. Leaves rustled above her as a soft breeze blew.

She walked over to the town's main attraction, The Devil's Lake. It was devastatingly breathtaking. The water shimmered even in the darkness, reflecting the pale moonlight.

A flood of memories came back to her mind.

She used to come here when she was five, with her mother. Her real mother. A strange shadow replaced her mother as she sat in her bedroom, telling her a bedtime story. It felt to her five-year-old self that nothing had happened. But now, as she stood by the glimmering lake, her memories seemed to have returned to her.

She pulled herself into the cold water as tears streamed down her cheeks. Her blonde locks turned to a light shade of ebony, and an intricate tail showed itself instead of her legs. It was decorated with turquoise scales that shone in the moonlight.

Adrenaline pumped through her veins. Somehow, she felt free, even after the disaster she had witnessed just moments ago.

She discovered something strange in the dark night, illuminated by the pale moonlight.

She was not human.

She had become something else.

It scared her, but at the same time, she felt the excitement of being unique.

Since the weather was calm in the forest, she didn't miss the sound of movement nearby. She turned around in the direction of the sound.

A woman, another one like her, entered the lake.

Beautiful was an understatement for the radiating aura she was. Her ebony hair was tied in an intricate braid. A few strands were loosened from the front, adding detail to her perfect jawline. Her sun-kissed skin glowed, giving her an almost angelic appearance.

Her sky-blue eyes looked curiously at Elizabeth, never leaving her eyes.

To Elizabeth, she somehow looked familiar, but she couldn't bring herself to pinpoint the resemblance.

The woman smiled at her, extended her hand to her in a friendly gesture, and smiled. She was a few inches apart from her, beckoning Elizabeth to come closer.

Elizabeth hesitated at first but then decided that

it might have been her mind playing games on her. For all she knew, she could've imagined the resemblance. Seeing it was impossible, she extended her arm, touching the woman's hand.

The woman's thin fingers brushed her bare arm until it stopped above her elbow. Her smile suddenly turned malicious as her grip around Elizabeth's arm tightened. Her eyes held a look of pure sadistic amusement.

Elizabeth's breath hitched in her throat. She felt something wrap around her legs, making its way over her body. She was wrapped in her tail. Her chest was throbbing with the piercing pain she felt. She clawed at her throat as she began to suffocate.

The woman smiled wickedly at her, enjoying the view of her writhing body.

Elizabeth could only stare at those pure black eyes. Eyes that held no emotion.

"Wherever you go, I'll find you, my love," the woman said as she dragged Elizabeth's half-dead body down to the lake's depths. A veil of black covered her vision until she couldn't see anymore. Until she couldn't feel her body anymore.

Elizabeth's eyes shot open as she took in sight around her. Cream-colored furniture lined the bright blue walls. Collages covered most of the space. A chandelier, a small one, hung from the ceiling. The sickeningly sweet smell of honey was lingering in the air.

As she realized it was her room, she sighed in relief. It was a dream.

She glanced at the clock. It read at am.

She had been getting those dreams lately. It's

the same dream all the time, but her death changes all the time. It troubled her. It was one of the main reasons she read at night.

She shouldn't have picked horror. It was a really bad choice with all the nightmares she was getting.

She stood up from her fluffy bed, took out all the horror stories from her shelf, and placed them in a hidden compartment so she wouldn't get tempted to read them. She knew it was a useless attempt, a subtle way of lying to herself.

How good her life would have been if she couldn't see the future before it happened.

Elizabeth was born with a strange gift. She could see the future in her dreams. She always thought of it as a blessing, but now that death started paying her visits, her gift looked like nothing but a curse. She had learned that the future could not be changed. If something was going to happen, she could've done nothing to stop it.

Once she was done placing the books inside, she yawned and stumbled onto her bed, forgetting about her worries, even if it was just for a few hours.

Once she was done placing the books inside, she let out a yawn and stumbled onto her bed, forgetting about her worries, even if it was just for a few hours. Her doorknob turned, and a fraction opened the door. A pair of black eyes were staring at Elizabeth's petite figure there.

The figure of an unknown woman entered her room silently. She slit her hand with her knife, then wrote a message for the beautiful girl sleeping on the bed.

After she was done, she walked back to the door, closing it carefully on her way out. She leaned against its cold wooden frame.

"Darling, I am coming for you. Soon. Very soon. Wait for me, my love," the woman whispered. She let out a throaty chuckle before locking the door from the outside and leaving a sleeping Elizabeth in her room. Elizabeth walked alongside the lockers of her high school, her legs trembling slightly, her confident gait gone. Last night's dream was still fresh in her memory. Her usually sparkling blue eyes looked dull and pale today. Her smile looked strained. She was wearing a rather normal outfit, not grabbing much attention from the teenagers roaming in the hallway.

Her hair was disheveled as if she had forgotten to comb it down. Dark circles loomed beneath her once radiant eyes. Anyone could tell that she had not been sleeping well lately. All it took was one look at her sorry state.

Elizabeth was horrified after she woke up today. Her room was too much to take in. And the news didn't help it at all. When she switched on the television this morning, she was greeted with a picture of a mutilated woman, a knife shoved into her chest, right where the heart was supposed to be. The mere sight of the body made her sick.

Then a video popped up. Detective Mary Parker and Alex Ricosta were standing at what Elizabeth supposed was the crime scene.

After what seemed to be an infinity, Detective Parker's voice greeted her ears.

"There have been a dangerous number of deaths in our town in the past few weeks. The victims were girls so far. There were no male deaths of this manner reported in this duration. The girls were brutally killed, and the lack of any major scars from bindings shows they were hopeful till their last minutes. They were then stabbed in the heart with a knife.

The murderer always leaves the knife behind. So far, we couldn't find anything about the killer. But we'll find him soon. That's my promise to you.

Until then, please don't go out with strangers. Don't date unknown men. It's not safe. You never know who this mysterious person could be."

When Detective Parker was finished, Detective Ricosta spoke up.

"I've seen many cases of homicide, but I've never seen one as bad as this. The killer has killed these girls mercilessly. We found a dead body yesterday night; the girl's name was June Summers.

She was found in an alleyway, killed by a stab to her heart. Many other injuries were also found. We couldn't connect with anyone close to June. So if you're watching this video and you know June, please come to the police station immediately."

Elizabeth remembered the news channel playing a slideshow containing pictures of the victims of the case after the video was over. They were all stabbed in their hearts. She felt sick as she watched them.

A bad feeling settled over her stomach. She felt nauseous and scared too. When she woke up today, she saw something shockingly horrible. A deep fear crawled up her body as she took in the sight of her blood-stained floor. A message was left for her there, written in a vicious red.

"I will come for you, love," it read.

The scent of iron nipped at her nostrils. She tried to shake off the image from her mind, trying to wake up from this nightmare. But this was reality. It surprised her how the mere smell of blood could affect her so much.

When she showed the message to her mother, she accused her of doing all this to get people's attention. She told her to stop doing such things and that she would not tolerate it if Elizabeth pulled a stunt like that again.

Her mother never loved Elizabeth.

Elizabeth's father had died the day she was born. He was coming to the hospital to see Elizabeth, but in his joy, he had failed to notice the car rushing towards him as he drove.

The driver was a drunk teenager who apparently had no idea of the world around him, one that had decided it would be a great idea to end his life by bumping into a car. The impact was so strong that it took both of their lives in seconds.

Though Elizabeth never got to see her father, her aunt used to tell her about him. He was a good man who treated everyone with love, and his life was really respected.

Her mother, however, never talked about her father with Elizabeth. Deep within her heart, she blamed Elizabeth for everything. Yet she wasn't the one to make her feel bad for it by accusing her of her father's death every now and then.

It surprised Elizabeth that a mother could be so cruel to her child.

To be truthful, she was afraid of her mother. Her life was an endless struggle. But she never gave up hope. She had always believed that something good would happen and life had started to turn better, but then death started visiting her on a daily basis.

At first, she thought it was probably nothing, but the nightmares started getting worse as time passed. She had convinced herself that it was nothing serious. But after today's incident, she knew for certain that something bad was going to happen to her. After all, her dreams were never false.

As she reached the cafeteria, her eyes started roaming everywhere, searching for her friends. She finally spotted them, sitting in the middle of the room, busy grabbing people's attention. She walked towards them.

Her friends greeted her, but she was too busy with her own thoughts. Grabbing Annie's hand, she left the table. Annie realized something was wrong with her best friend, so she told the girls they'd be back in a few minutes.

Annie stayed quiet as Elizabeth led the way, never once letting go.

When they reached a fairly secluded area, Elizabeth took a deep breath and told Annie everything that had happened in the past month.

Annie looked fairly confused at first, but then the real possibilities of the situation began to dawn on her.

She was sure that Elizabeth's life was in danger. Annie patted her back gently.

Elizabeth couldn't hold it anymore. She started crying. One by one, tears fell from her eyes. Annie slowly caressed her best friend's cheek.

"We are going to the police station. Now," she said.

When she saw that Elizabeth was still crying, it broke her heart. "Don't worry. We'll figure this out together. Here, drink some water," she said, handing her a fresh water bottle.

Elizabeth drank it without any complaint. Her throat was dry from all the crying. The cold water soothed her throat.

"Let's do this," she said firmly.

They bunked the school together. Elizabeth had never bunked school in her whole life. She was worried about getting caught, but they got out of the school borders without much problem.

They took a bus to the police station after walking for a few minutes. Elizabeth's heart thundered within her chest as they sat on the bus. Her breaths were labored. Her palms were getting sweaty.

Annie gently took her hand in hers and started telling her a story.

"Once upon a time, a beautiful girl lived in a town with her mother. Her mother always treated the girl badly because she blamed the girl for her husband's death.

The girl wasn't loved by her family, but she had some great friends. All of her friends adored her. She was so beautiful, after all. All the boys were crazy for her. But she didn't give them much attention.

The girl had a friend she had learned to call her best friend. They both were happy when they were with each other. They supported each other through every crisis. They even made cute boyfriends together."

Elizabeth couldn't help but laugh. The last part made her giggle. Annie laughed alongside her.

"What happened next?" Elizabeth asked, suddenly interested in the story.

"We'll save that part for later," Annie said in a light voice.

After a while, the bus stopped near the police station. As they got off the bus, they started walking towards the police station.

Annie saw Elizabeth's mother at the police station. She motioned Elizabeth to look. As Elizabeth looked at her mother's familiar figure, she was drowned in a deep sense of fear.

What was her mother doing there? She wasn't supposed to be here. She was meant to be at the hospital at that time, doing her job as a nurse.

She grabbed Annie's hand so tightly that her blood stopped. Annie was sure that it was going to get bruised later.

"Beth, you're hurting me," Annie whispered in pain.

As Elizabeth realized what she was doing, she let go of Annie's hand and mumbled an apology.

"Let's go there sometime later. Wanna go to Starbucks?" she asked, trying to lighten the mood.

Annie was more than aware of Elizabeth and

her mother's fragile relationship.

Somehow, Annie felt that her mother was behind all this. She stopped herself from mentioning the possibility to Elizabeth in mid-sentence. Elizabeth stared at her quizzically.

Annie decided that it'd be best if she didn't know. It would worry her, after all. She decided to keep a close eye on them.

"Starbucks? Sure," mumbled a tired Elizabeth, "but you're going to pay."

Annie chuckled slightly and rolled her eyes at her best friend's childish behavior.

They entered the fairly crowded Starbucks. They walked around and sat on one of the far corners of the shop to avoid much attention. Annie ordered a latte, while Elizabeth ordered a chocolate mocha.

The whole mattress thing was forgotten, even just for a small amount of time, as the two best friends talked about their friends and classmates. Chitter-chatter and laughter filled the air as they both talked. Annie sure knew how to lighten Elizabeth's mood.

When it was time for Annie to leave, she bid farewell to Elizabeth and made her way outside to the bus stop.

Elizabeth watched Annie leave. Her mind was filled with clouds of worry. Her eyes looked hazy all of a sudden.

She thought that she was going to pass out.

She ran to the restroom. Then vomited the contents of her stomach.

The strong smell of vomit made her feel sick.

She covered her nose with her handkerchief to avoid it as much as possible.

Her head was aching. After cleaning up, she returned to her table and ordered a coffee.

From the corner of her eye, she saw a dark figure standing behind her, watching her closely. Elizabeth turned around, but there was no one in sight.

Must be daydreaming, she thought as she went back to drinking her coffee.

Elizabeth stayed in Starbucks for another hour or so since she didn't want to go home and confront her mother. She wondered what her mother had been doing at the police station.

Was she following her? She wondered about that question for a moment. Her body stiffened at the thought of it.

Seeing as it was getting dark outside, she decided to leave and catch a bus home. She was still a bit queasy about seeing her mother.

A woman was sitting in her car, tapping her manicured fingers on the steering wheel. A woman was sitting in her car, tapping her manicured fingers on the steering wheel. Her eyes were fixed on the sidewalk as a blonde girl walked towards the bus stop. The blonde stopped midway in her path, talking to an old friend of hers. The woman's desire to taste her blood was tempting, but she waited patiently, not wanting to scare her target away.

After all, Elizabeth Scottson was a girl worth waiting for.

Elizabeth climbed on the bus. She walked over

to an old lady, smiling at her as she decided to take the seat. Before she could sit down, a folded piece of paper lying on the seat caught her attention.

She picked it up.

She unfolded it slowly, cautiously reading the note.

She read it again, and again until the words were drilled into her memory.

"I am coming for you, love."

Elizabeth couldn't think straight. Her life had become a toy to this killer. A nightmare she could never escape from. She felt an attack lingering around the corner, but she managed to keep it at bay.

In a state of deep fear, she scanned the bus with her eyes. Her eyes landed on a familiar figure she had seen too many times. He was really famous for his work.

Elizabeth went straight to him.

Detective Ricosta was startled by the sudden pull on his hand. He looked behind to see a young girl holding her wrist. He wondered how a little girl could have such a strong grip.

"I need your help," she said, looking him straight in the eye. Alex wondered how daring she was to keep looking him straight in the eye. He eyed her fingers, millimeters away from clawing through his skin. Realizing she had been holding his wrist, Elizabeth let it go. She pulled her hand back.

"And what might such a young girl needs help with, except for asking about the latest fashion of clothes? If that is what you are here about, I am sorry, but I can't help you," he said, trying to get rid of the girl.

He was way too tired and agitated from the case he had been dealing with. He didn't have time for girls who sought people's attention. There were more than so many reasons to deny the girl.

He had his fair share of young girls trying to hit on him. He was tired of it, and this beautiful girl with those curious blue eyes was no exception.

The girl glared at Alex as if he had just insulted her, indirectly calling her a slut. Alex scrutinized the girl for a second before sighing deeply.

"What do you want?" he asked, meeting the gaze of her pale blue eyes. The girl took a deep breath.

"I think someone is stalking me. I am getting these letters everywhere I go. First, I got this message on my floor written with blood, and now on the seat where I would sit. I'm just scared. I- I don't know what to do!" she said breathlessly as she handed him the folded piece of paper she held so carefully in her hands.

Elizabeth felt a sudden wave of suffocation. She placed her hand on her chest, taking slow breaths to calm down.

He took it from her and read it. It didn't surprise him. The girl standing before him was so beautiful that anyone could have decided to stalk her.

"You should inform your parents about this," he said.

"My mother won't believe me..."

Detective Ricosta knew that he had touched the wrong string. He quickly changed the subject.

"Well then, you could report a complaint. The cops might be able to help you. He might be a lover messing with you," he said.

"You don't understand. It isn't a man that's behind this; it's a woman. And she wants to kill me!" she yelled, suddenly getting all hyped up. Her palms started sweating; her breath now labored as she tried to stand her ground. She was having an attack. Again.

Elizabeth bit her tongue. Her luck had always been rotten to the core.

Elizabeth felt her knees buckling. Her vision had begun to fail her, slowly starting to whirl all over the place. Sounds came to her in echoes, rippling through the atmosphere as if they had been shot through a cone. Elizabeth held onto a pole in an attempt to keep her composure. The girl tried to cover it up with a smile, not letting the detective know.

Her hand began to tremble. This was not going well.

Elizabeth took a deep breath as casually as she could, trying to keep her fits of suffocation at bay.

However, the ignorance of the man in front of her ended it. She felt as though he wasn't paying the slightest bit of attention to her problem. Panic had given way to a fair amount of anger. He was no different than the rest.

Alex thought that the girl had gone mad. He shook his head at her behavior. It was really unusual for someone to send her such notes, but what was more unusual was that the girl knew who it was and what the person wanted. That just couldn't have been possible. It could have been an attempt to grab his attention for all he knew.

"I can't help you, I'm really sorry," he said as he turned around. From the corner of his eye, he saw the girl cursing under her breath as she went to sit on her seat.

Without getting noticed by anyone, he took out his cell phone and clicked a picture of the girl. As immoral as it may be, he could not ignore his intuition. He sent it to his partner, Detective Mary, to do a background check on her, just in case. He didn't believe the girl completely, though. She had to be lying.

It rained that day. Elizabeth didn't have an umbrella, but it wasn't like she cared anyway. She walked silently in the pattern of raindrops, not even trying to keep herself warm. She wanted to feel the deadening cold bite at her skin. She wanted to feel each and every ounce of the pain it offered. Such was the burden of one who'd been branded a liar.

She shoved the key into its hole, nearly breaking the lock in her anger. With a shallow click, Elizabeth unlocked the door to her old house, tears falling from her face. Her carpets had become a soggy mess as the girl stood there silently. She clenched her fists. Being helpless had become routine these days.

Elizabeth was scared. She tried to tell Detective Ricosta, but he shrugged her off as if she was lying.

It hurt her. It wasn't a surprise, though.

No one ever believed her. She had always been the bad girl in people's eyes. She was always neglected because of her anger issues. Teachers, classmates, sometimes even her friends. They'd all stay away from her using one reason or the other. By the time she changed herself, the visions had begun to kick in.

It had become the seed of a whole new reason for people to avoid her. And thus, she was branded a liar.

Elizabeth knew that telling her mother was not a good idea. She was only going to get blamed.

She wished her father would be there for her at times like these. How good would it have felt if her father was still alive! Her mother would have loved her. Her father would've comforted her when she was in trouble. Fathers do that, don't they?

But life had a different plan for Elizabeth; it wanted to make her suffer. It didn't want her to be happy. Whenever she earned a little happiness, it was taken away from her.

At that moment, Elizabeth realized that being happy was the worst feeling ever.

Because happiness is something that can be snatched away from you in seconds...

Elizabeth went inside her room and locked the door. She lay on her bed, the day's events resurfacing in her mind. The note, Detective Alex's rejection, her upcoming death. It was all too much. She let out a muffled sob as she held cried into her soft pillow. She would have done anything to get out of there, to be normal. But there was nothing she could do. She was helpless.

Elizabeth's eyes were filled to the rim with tears, her psyche at the edge of a breakdown.

It was then that her phone rang. She sat up on her bed. Wiping her face with the back of her hand, she picked up the phone to check who was calling her.

It was an unknown number. Before Elizabeth could have picked the phone, the call ended. Her phone dinged, notifying her that a message had been sent to her.

She opened the message. It was the same unknown number. It had an attachment to it. Her eyes widened as she read the words flashing on her screen. She threw her phone away from herself, horrified.

It was a picture of her lying in her bed, crying. The words "You look good, Love" were written on the picture.

Elizabeth ran out of her room, flinging her phone onto the bed.

No matter how bad her mother was, Elizabeth needed her.

Elizabeth knocked on her mother's door loudly. She kept on doing it till her mother opened the door. A very annoyed Edna was standing in front of Elizabeth.

"What do you want? I told you not to disturb me while I'm sleeping. Doesn't anything get through that thick head of yours? If you got a nightmare, it doesn't matter. Everyone gets them. You don't have to make a big deal out of it. Now go away!" she said with her eyes closed.

However, when she looked at her daughter's face, she knew something was amiss. She wanted to ask her what was wrong but couldn't bring herself to do so. The guilt was too much.

She remembered her horrible past whenever she looked at her daughter's face. All she saw was her husband. He had left her.

As she looked at her daughter, a sudden tide of hate rose in her chest.

"You need to grow up. When will you ever stop being such a bother? You always create trouble. Look at you, crying like a small child who lost her toy. Get out of my sight before I'll say something I'll regret," she bellowed.

A look of pain flashed in her daughter's eyes. "But mother...," she started, only to be cut off by Edna's piercing words. "Out, now!"

Elizabeth sobbed loudly before she ran off to her father's room.

Edna missed her husband. He was so loving. He loved Edna to such an extent that it made her cry.

Even after hearing the news of her pregnancy, his love never dwindled for her once. She missed him so much. Even after everything, she wanted to love her daughter but couldn't find it in herself to love her.

Elizabeth shut the door behind her. This room was the only place in the house where she didn't feel lonely.

Somehow, she could feel the loving presence of her father in the room. She looked at the single photo frame of her father that sat beside his bed. Her eyes were puffy from crying.

"Why did you leave? Was it even necessary? I miss you, father. Please come back," she pleaded as she looked at the photo frame, tears falling from her eyes. "I'm so scared. Please come back..."

Elizabeth felt a warmth in her chest. She felt as if her father was there, even if it was just for a few seconds. After such a long time, she felt safe. The sense of comfort, however, was gone as soon as it came.

A sudden wave of dread washed over her body.

From the corner of her eye, she saw a note being slid inside from under her door. This was not happening. She must have been dreaming. Not again.

She grabbed the railing of the bed. She gulped as she felt paranoia trickling down her spine. Elizabeth's body trembled as she cautiously walked towards the door, not daring to make a noise. She bent down and picked up the note.

It can't be...

She dropped the note as soon as she opened it. She tried to turn the doorknob, but the door was locked from the outside. She screamed and thrashed the door, but it was of no use.

Her throat was dry, and nothing but scratchy sounds came out of her mouth. No one would be able to hear her. She fell to her knees, sobbing loudly. Her throat was sore; her body was aching. Her mother was in danger.

"I'm coming for you, love, but I need to handle your mother first. Then, it'll be only you and me. Together for eternity."

She cried against the door for what felt like an eon. The door never opened. And in the dark gaze of the night, she lost her consciousness.

Marina Denver was sitting on one of the seats of

the local bar of the town

Marina Denver was sitting on one of the town's local bar seats. The one on the outskirts was the only bar she went to.

Dressed in a beautiful royal blue gown, she looked nothing but attractive. Boys and men were checking her out, but she was unaware of their gazes fixed on her.

A man in his mid-twenties came towards her. He looked at her, his eyes never leaving her face.

"Wanna go out with me, honeybun?" he said, his voice lowly and drunk.

Marina shook her head, disgusted by the man. She stood up and left the bar to get some fresh air.

She saw a dark figure standing in the shadows of the night. The figure turned around slightly and faced Marina. Marina smiled at the woman.

"Can I come to your place tonight?" she asked, her voice trembling slightly.

"Sure, come with me," Marina said as she opened the car door.

The woman smiled as she saw her figure. She looked amazing. Her blood looked inviting.

She knew tonight's meal would be exquisite.

You are not beautiful. Look at you. You are nothing compared to her! Get out of my sight," the boy said while facing the woman.

The woman's delicate fingers had curled into a fist. She looked at the girl he was pointing at.

There, at the far table of the shop, Elizabeth was sitting with her friend, Marina. They seemed to be chatting.

The woman's blood boiled in anger as she saw

Elizabeth. He had his finger pointed at her.

She stood up from the chair and walked towards Elizabeth.

Both Elizabeth and Marina smiled as they saw her coming towards them. Before they could say anything, the woman plunged a fork sitting on the table right into Elizabeth's throat.

The searing sensation of pain struck fear in Elizabeth's heart. Her breathing grew erratic as blood oozed from her throat. Marina shrieked loudly, horrified.

The woman laughed evilly as she saw Elizabeth dying in front of her eyes.

A gasp escaped Elizabeth's lips.

Her eyes opened slightly. Where was she?

As she finally opened her eyes, incidents of last night flashed by in her memory.

Her head was throbbing. She felt a burning sensation in her throat. She tried to speak, but no words came out.

She grabbed the doorknob and tried to stand up but failed miserably. Her foot caught on something, and she fell to the floor with a loud thud.

A misty haze of white surrounded her vision. She was unable to see anything. She tried to stand again, but no strength was left within her body.

Her eyes fluttered closed as she struggled to hold on to the last of her conscience.

Her eyes fluttered closed as she struggled to hold on to the last of her conscience.
Detective Alex Ricosta ordered a cup of coffee.

A soft yawn escaped his lips. He was studying the case of Madeline Denver, who was found dead in her room by her parents. She had been stabbed in the heart.

Detective Mary handed him the background files of Madeline Denver.

He opened the file, looking through the list of persons associated with Miss Denver. It was then that a certain name caught his attention.

Elizabeth Scottson.

The girl whom he had met on the bus. The same mysterious yet so appealing girl whom he had mistaken for a troublemaker.

He had pulled her background files, too, to find any helpful information about her, but there was nothing else. She was just another one of those ordinary high school girls.

His brow creased with surprise as he looked at her name in Miss Denver's file. He knew that Elizabeth was not normal, he had felt it when he was talking to her on the bus.

She knew many things. Detective Alex wondered for a moment if Elizabeth was behind all this.

He shrugged the thought away. The killer was a man, and he knew that. Yet, he was unable to shake off her image. Her words were playing over and over in his mind.

Something about this case was missing, and Elizabeth was his only hope of finding it out. He rushed out of the office before his coffee even arrived.

He opened the door to his car and drove off to Elizabeth's house. He needed answers, and only she could provide them.

As he pulled up at her address, a large Victorian house greeted his eyes. He turned off his car and got out.

He climbed the steps to the porch and rang the bell. A subtle chime filled the air. After a few seconds, the door was opened. A middle-aged woman stood at the entrance.

She wore an apron around her waist but didn't fail to look beautiful even in simple clothes.

Detective Alex didn't fail to notice the striking similarity between her and Elizabeth. They were both alike with their beautiful features and petite frames.

"Who are you?" she asked him gently.

"I'm Detective Alex Ricosta. I've come to see Miss Scottson. Is she home?" he asked her.

At the mention of Elizabeth's name, her mother's eyes suddenly grew dark.

"That I'm not aware of, but I'll check. Come inside, please."

She made Detective Ricosta sit on the couch while she went to Elizabeth's room to check on her.

Alex thought about how uncaring her mother was. She didn't know where her daughter was at all.

She returned from her room and offered him a glass of water.

"I'm sorry, but Elizabeth isn't home," said the lady.

Knowing that Elizabeth's mother was useless to him, he decided to leave. He picked up his keys from the coffee table.

When he reached the door, he heard a strange

noise coming from somewhere. He stopped midway in turning the doorknob. He looked around.

The noise was faint, as if someone was trying to knock on the door but didn't have the strength to do so. His eyes roamed around, locking on the source of the sound. He walked past the woman in front of him. It felt like there was no time for etiquette anymore.

A very confused Mrs.Scottson looked at Detective Alex, not appealed by his sudden reaction. She followed his gait regardless.

As he stepped in front of Mr. Scottson's room, her hand involuntarily reached for his. She pulled his hand away, stopping him from opening the door.

Detective Alex yanked his hand away from her, turning the doorknob quickly before Mrs. Scottson could retort.

The door made a creaking noise as he opened it. Detective Alex chose to enter the room despite Mrs. Scottson's protests.

The detective gasped in shock.

He ran over to Elizabeth, placing his hands under her head. She was lying on the floor, barely conscious. He picked her up in his arms and put her on the bed.

When Mrs. Scottson saw Detective Alex carrying Elizabeth, she ran to her side.

"Water," Elizabeth murmured. Her voice was so dry that, for a moment, no one understood what she was trying to say.

Listening to her hoarse voice, Detective Alex

ran to the kitchen to fetch water.

He made Elizabeth drink the water. All the while, he noticed the raged expression on Mrs. Scottson's face. He knew she was angry. What he didn't understand was what was making her so angry all of a sudden.

Elizabeth noticed her too, and caught her breath. She gripped Detective Alex's arm tightly.

Detective Alex was beyond convinced that something was wrong with Elizabeth and her mother.

After Elizabeth recovered from her state, he asked her what had happened. It was a hard task, but he managed to send Mrs. Scottson out of the room.

Once they were alone, Elizabeth started describing what had happened in a frenzy. She told him everything from how she had gone to his dad's study to how someone locked her from the outside.

After getting all the necessary information, Detective Alex Ricosta bid her farewell.

As he walked back to his car, he couldn't help but think that somehow Mrs. Scottson was behind all of it. It was all so possible that it didn't fail to get noticed.

A man was leaning against the hood of his car, eyeing the Victorian house carefully

A man was leaning against the hood of his car, eyeing the Victorian house carefully.

He had seen the Detective leave. Now that he was sure they were alone, he exited his car.

As he looked at the house, a sudden urge went through his body. He couldn't wait. It was time to appear, whether someone liked it or not.

He left his car and walked the steps of the house. It was all his, after all. She was his.

Alex hadn't mentioned anything about Madeline since there was so much going on in the Scottson household already

Alex hadn't mentioned anything about Madeline since there was so much going on in the Scottson household already. He couldn't bear to add to Elizabeth's misfortune. He wondered what kind of life the girl led, abandoned by her father and scorned by her mother.

A sudden ring brought him back to reality. It was his phone.

He checked the caller Id. It was Detective Parker. He wondered why she was calling him.

He picked up the phone, realizing that it must have been urgent.

"I need you at the Avalon apartments, Mayfair, second street. We've found a dead body inside the room," said Mary.

"Details, Detective."

"The name's Jessica Miles. Skin decayed. Smells awful. Looks like the crime took place three days ago. Her neighbors were on a trip, and when they came back, they smelled something foul coming from her room. So they decided to check. When they found the girl's dead body, they immediately contacted the police."

"I'll be there within the hour," said detective Ricosta as he got in his car, driving full-throttle towards Avalon apartments.

Elizabeth was lying on the bed, her back

supported against the headboard. Her mother was looking at her, enraged.

Elizabeth had never seen her mother so angry before. She was trembling under her ferocious gaze. Her mother opened her mouth to say something, but the doorbell cut her off.

Seeing as she wasn't going to open the gate herself, Elizabeth went to check who was there.

When Elizabeth opened the door, her eyes met with sparkly blue ones, just like her. The man looked at her in admiration.

"Hello, sir. Do you need anything?" she asked him.

Before he could say anything, her mother shrieked shrilly. She was shouting at the man to get out of her house, about how he wasn't invited here.

Elizabeth looked at her mom and then at the man. They were contrasting each other. While her mother was red with anger, the man remained calm and uncaring.

Suddenly, Elizabeth was yanked back by her mother. The man walked inside the house, closing the door behind him.

Elizabeth felt fear.

The man didn't seem like good news to her. Not to mention that he had locked them inside.

Her mother screamed at him, trying to get him out.

He didn't even flinch as she tried to push him over.

"Why don't you tell her the truth, Edna? It'll help her if anything. You cannot keep secrets from your daughter. It's not right," he said, his gaze fixed on Elizabeth.

Edna screamed in defiance as she tried to push him away. He grabbed her arms and held it back. Before Elizabeth could've reacted, he spoke up.

"I, Maxon Montgomery, am your father, Elizabeth."

"W-What?"

Elizabeth's face turned pale. She grabbed a nearby chair to stop herself from falling.

As the man in front of her saw that she wasn't going to say anything, he let go of Edna's arm.

Elizabeth knew that he wasn't her father. Her father's name was Jake Scottson, not Maxon Montgomery. Besides, the pictures in her father's room weren't even close to resembling the man standing before her.

"I don't believe you. You're lying," she said while trying to control herself from stuttering.

"I know that this may sound weird to you, but I'm your real father. Your mother and I were together before she married the man you think of as your parent," he said, taking a step towards her.

"Your mother was pregnant with our child but kept it a secret from me. Jake isn't your father, I am. I've come to rescue you, Elizabeth. Come with me, my daughter."

By the time he was finished, his eyes were moist.

Tears brimmed at the corner of his eyes, but he blinked them back quickly.

Elizabeth wanted to run towards him, to claim him as her father. All her life, the only thing she ever wanted was a father. And there he was, welcoming her with open hands. Before she could make a move, her mother cut into the silence.

"She's my daughter. You have no right over her. I'm not going to give her to you. Get out of my house! Otherwise, I'll call the police," she screamed at him.

"She's my daughter too. I have the same rights over her as you. Don't act as if you care, Edna. I bet you don't even give her the love she deserves. Please give her back to me. I'm begging you, Edna. Please..."

"There's no way I'm letting it happen. Do you even know..."

Elizabeth's temper was slowly rising as she tried to tune out their conversation. It was all way too much for her.

First that knowing she was going to die soon, then all this. It was taking a toll on her.

"Shut it!"

The room grew silent as her voice bellowed loudly. Both the elders looked at her, anticipating her answer. She looked at them for a moment, a scowl on her lips.

"I need some time to think. Please leave me alone for some time. "

Knowing it wouldn't do any good, Maxon left the house without uttering another word. Her mother didn't move.

With heavy steps, Elizabeth retired to her room. She looked in the mirror. She was slowly starting to pity herself.

"I... have a father..."

All she wanted to do was cry, but she kept

herself back from doing so.

Her mother suddenly came in without knocking. As Elizabeth looked at her, she noticed that her mother's eyes were not uncaring like usual. Today, they were devoid of any emotions.

"You are not going anywhere with him. If he asks for you, tell him you won't come with him. That's my order," she said in a really low voice.

"Whatever he said, was it true, mother?", Elizabeth asked with a hint of uncertainty in her voice.

"Yes. Yes, it is. But you are not going anywhere. It is decided."

And with that, she was gone. As she banged the door close, something inside Elizabeth also broke.

Once again, the people she cared about were snatched away from her life. Her world was shattering beneath her feet.

All she could do was wait as it fell to oblivion.

Maxon walked back to his car, enraged at the encounter

Maxon walked back to his car, enraged at the encounter. Edna wouldn't even let Elizabeth come with him, even though she was his own daughter.

But there was no way he was going to let it happen.

Elizabeth was his daughter, his only daughter. He was definitely going to take her back with him, whatever it took.

Elizabeth's eyes looked dull and lifeless. She was in the front seat of her Literature class, interested neither in her surroundings nor her teacher's words.

It had been two days since she found out that she had a father. Two achingly long days.

Her father hadn't visited since.

She should have been happy after hearing the news of her father, but somehow, her thoughts were turning a shade darker than usual. She felt a storm of emotions swirling down her soul.

The shrill ring of the bell brought her back to reality.

It was recess.

Annie was absent today, so Elizabeth was feeling the world weighing down on her shoulders.

After the class had left, she sat alone in the monumentally placed, haphazardly structured benches of Room Thirteen.

After a few minutes, she got up from her seat. She walked out of the classroom, making her way toward the corridor. Instead of taking a left to go to the mess hall, she took a right.

After a few steps, she took another right turn. Another right once again.

She was finally there. She spotted an empty parking space as she walked out of the parking lot.

The space where Marina's car was supposed to be.

The principal had arranged an assembly for the students in the morning, where he informed everyone about the news of Marina's death. A veil of silence and sadness loomed over the school.

After a few hours, Marina was erased from everyone's memory. Forgotten. Erased from existence. Elizabeth felt sick as she looked at the empty space. She turned around, walking towards the exit.

A soft yawn escaped her lips. She hadn't slept properly for the past few days.

Nightmares of her death haunted her frequently, growing less bearable with each passing night. And then, there was her father.

Elizabeth walked as far away from her school as possible. The place had now become a monument of her misery, reminding her of everything from her vivid nightmares to the death of her friend. She needed solace.

Elizabeth spotted a coffee shop by the pavement that had recently become famous for its eccentric name and an even more eccentric menu. Demon's Coffee, read the sign. Elizabeth sighed as she walked towards it.

As soon as she entered, the chime of the doorbell rang in a sweet monotony, notifying her presence to the people around her.

She silently took a seat in the corner of the shop, avoiding as much attention as she could. Soon, a waitress came by to take her order. She placed the menu on the table.

Elizabeth scanned through the menu, not interested at all. She closed the menu book slowly and let her eyes wander.

As she looked at different people sitting in the coffee shop, her eyes caught on one familiar person.

It was him. It had to be him.

Elizabeth got up from her seat in excitement. She went towards his table. His eyes were carefully scrutinizing a newspaper. Sitting in front of her was none other than Detective Alex Ricosta.

She took a seat across from him, hoping to elicit some sort of response. Hearing the clatter of the chair, Detective Ricosta looked up, only to be greeted by the sight of a pale, exhausted teenager with eyes of sparkling blue.

Elizabeth.

"Hello, Detective," she said, greeting him with a warm smile.

"Elizabeth? Why are you here?" he asked her with a hint of uncertainty in his voice.

"I believe that whatever you came to say to me back then must have been important. I don't think you'd remember me otherwise," she laced her courteous words with a hint of sarcasm.

"I believe you are right about that.", he said, playing along trying to avoid the expected question as much as possible.

"So, why did you want to meet me? Any special reasons, Detective?" she asked.

"Elizabeth, I'm really sorry. Your friend Marina, I believe she is no longer among us. She was killed by a serial killer. The one who has been stabbing people in the heart."

Elizabeth felt her mind stop for a few minutes. She could no longer make out Detective Ricosta's words. They seemed jumbled up all of a sudden.

It was the woman that killed her. She was going to kill Elizabeth too.

"Elizabeth, are you even listening to me?" asked Detective Ricosta, snapping his fingers in front of her face.

"Yes...I'm listening. Continue, detective," she

said in a monotonous voice. He opened his mouth to speak but stopped as he noticed Elizabeth wanted to say something.

She shook her head at him, urging him to continue.

"Elizabeth, I know that you know something about the case. You know something, but you're keeping it from everyone. Look, I've seen those dead girls. The killer took their lives without the slightest hint of mercy. He deserves to be punished."

"It's not a he; it's a she," Elizabeth cut in.

"How do you..."

After a moment's pause, he spoke again, "How do you know? Is there something you are hiding from us, Elizabeth?"

A deep silence hung in the air. Elizabeth opened her mouth to say something, but words didn't come out.

"No, I'm not hiding anything from you. And I know that it's a woman because I saw her. I saw her in an alleyway, with a dead girl lying next to her, a knife plunged in her heart."

Alex took in the information. It was hard to believe Elizabeth. He knew she was lying about the part about seeing the woman in an alleyway.

"Which alleyway?" he asked tactfully.

"Madison Avenue. Time of death: in the afternoon. The body was found in the alley of the Town Building in the southern corner. Satisfied?" she asked.

Detective Alex nodded as he let out a sigh of defeat.

He stood up from his chair and gave Elizabeth a hand. Elizabeth took it and stood up.

"Come, I'll drop you home," he said, letting go of her hand.

"You? You yourself were traveling in public transport the last time I met you," she teased, trying to lighten the tension in the air.

Alex rubbed the back of his neck shyly. "Well, my car got a little malfunction a few days ago. So, I had no option but to use public transport. Now it's repaired, and you're coming with me. End of story."

Elizabeth chuckled lightly before following him outside the coffee shop.

A soft silence hung calmly in the car as they drove. No one said anything, but both of them had a smile on their faces.

Once they reached Elizabeth's home, Detective Ricosta stopped the car. They both got out of the car.

"Come in," Elizabeth says all of a sudden.

Detective Ricosta followed her inside. She guided him to sit on the couch.

"I'll be back in a few minutes; wait here," she said, motioning him to stay put.

She went upstairs to her room in a hurry. She got in and pulled some stuff from her drawer.

With much creating of her eyebrows, she wrote down something on the paper with her pen.

She didn't know what motivated her to write all that, but one thing she felt sure of was that she trusted Detective Ricosta.

It would be an understatement to say that writing all that was a hard task.

After Elizabeth was finished, she folded the long paper and put it inside the envelope she had found lying around.

She left her door open as she walked downstairs to where he was sitting.

He got up and walked to her. Seeing the envelope in her hands, a look of concern took over his features.

"I have to give something to you. But you have to promise me something first. Promise me that you won't open it until I ask you to do so. Promise?" she asked.

"I promise you that I won't open it unless and until you ask me to," he said, repeating her words with a genuine smile.

Elizabeth slowly handed the letter. He took it from her eagerly.

"Okay, you can go now before my mother comes."

Alex nodded his head as he left the house. He smiled widely as the door closed behind him.

He had gotten a clue. He knew it. Elizabeth was stupid to think he would wait for her permission to open the envelope.

He slowly tore the lining.

Solving this case meant everything to him. He could stop this streak of murders. He could punish the guilty. His thoughts were justified regardless of how he looked at them.

Yet something stirred inside him.

He couldn't bring himself to open the letter. With a sigh, he put it back.

"Guess I'll have to wait then."

Black clothes lined the clearance as far as one could see. Everyone had a black umbrella in hand. The sound of raindrops echoed loudly as they fell on the umbrellas, dripping to the ground soon after.

Mother nature wept upon Marina Denver's death.

A huge podium was set on the ground in order to give speeches. The graveyard looked lively once again with all the people inside, yet it did nothing to undo the sadness of untimely death.

There in the middle was Marina's coffin, her final bed in which she lay ever so peacefully. Her parents were nearby, crying in anguish, unable to control themselves from the grief of their lost daughter.

Everyone around them tried to comfort them. Edna and Annie were there, too, trying to comfort Mrs. Denver with all their strength. Everything looked disastrous in their town.

The minister had come. He gave a long speech about Marina's death, a speech that sent her off with a reminder of her good memories and the lives she touched. A speech that did honor to her existence.

Once he was done, it was Elizabeth's turn to give a few words about her friend.

With trembling legs, she walked up to the podium. Her hands trembled as she touched the microphone placed there temporarily for a speech session.

She took a deep breath and wiped her eyes before bringing her mouth close to the microphone.

"Marina Denver was such a sweet girl. Even

sugar failed in comparison." Elizabeth couldn't help but smile from the warm memories that flooded her heart.

"She came into my life accidentally, purely by God's mere joke. Some bullies had tied my legs together and pushed me down the stairs.

"Then, like an angel, she appeared out of nowhere and stopped me from falling to my death. God knew I was a clumsy kid back then. Then started our bittersweet friendship. I was always the bad child, and yet she always tried to bring out the good in me." Elizabeth paused for a second. It was hard to keep her composure.

"I can't believe that this happened to her. I can't believe I'm not going to see her ever again, to see her sweet smile again. It hurts me to even think about it. Marina Denver was a great friend, a sweet daughter, and an extraordinary girl. She'll be forever in my heart, and I know she'll be yours too. Thank you for being my friend, Marina. I'll never be able to forget it. Not in a million years."

As she finished, the audience was in tears. She walked down the podium to Marina's coffin and placed a pink rose on it. She bent down, whispering into her friend's cold, lifeless ears.

"I'm sorry for what happened to you, Marina. Rest in peace."

Elizabeth walked away, a solitary tear falling down her cheek.

Soon, everyone was placing roses on her coffin. Once all the people had placed their roses, everyone turned silent as they closed their eyes and uttered a silent prayer for Marina Denver.

All of a sudden, a blood-curdling scream filled the air. The people turned towards the sound, wide-eyed from a mixture of panic and fear.

Suddenly, a girl wearing a black dress ran out from the bushes. A few of the guests ran to her aid, the rest standing frozen in terror. They watched as the girl pointed her finger to the forest, her arms trembling in fear. Her words were beyond comprehension. All they could make out were gasps of shock.

Elizabeth looked at her skeptically, following the guests into the forest anyway.

By now, a majority of the people had entered the forest, determined to see the reason for the girl's scream.

A few meters into the forest, Elizabeth heard a gasp. She rushed forward, catching up to the people ahead of her in no time. The guests had crowded by a bush's side. Elizabeth squeezed her way to the front. What she saw shocked her.

Lying in front of them was the body, a knife plugged into her heart. Another victim of the serial killer, the same one that got Marina.

The fresh scent of iron was nauseating. Elizabeth couldn't breathe.

The crowd gasped in horror as they stepped back, watching a pool of viscous red spreading toward them.

Elizabeth couldn't believe what she saw in front of her. The girl's face looked so warm, so alive. Yet how could her eyes be so blank?

She felt a pang of pain searing through her chest.

They had just witnessed a live murder. The killer had been there just minutes ago.

Elizabeth fumbled around her jeans. She pulled out her phone, unlocking the pattern after a few attempts had gone wrong.

With trembling fingers, she dialed Alex's number. A few rings passed before a hoarse voice answered the call.

"Hello, this is Detective Ricosta speaking."

"Detective, Alex. It's me, Elizabeth. I'm at Marina's funeral. We have a dead body over here. Come fast. Please," she informed him, stuttering in between her words.

"I'll be there right now. You stay put," he said as he hung up the call.

Elizabeth put her phone back in her pocket, crouching down to the body to see the girl's face. Her breath was pulled short as she noticed the face of the girl.

It was Jane Samson, a friend Elizabeth held dearly. A friend who happened to be Marina's best friend too.

Tears escaped her eyes as she started sobbing loudly. Elizabeth struggled to look at her friend's corpse. She felt her stomach wrench as she looked at the knife lodged in her heart.

She heard a loud gasp behind her, followed by hysterical cries of despair. It didn't take her long to realize that it was Jane's mother.

Her mother was crying loudly behind Elizabeth. Her husband arrived soon, lost in grief as he looked at his daughter's mutilated body.

"Police! Please stand back from the crime

scene."

The detectives had arrived. Alex came there with Detective Mary by his side.

Detective Parker went to search the body for any clue of evidence while Detective Ricosta tried to calm down a sobbing Elizabeth. She looked like a mess, her hair sticking to her face because of the sheen of sweat on her forehead.

He slowly put her hair behind her neck and offered her a handkerchief.

Elizabeth seemed to have stopped crying by then. He offered her a water bottle he had asked Detective Parker for. Elizabeth took it and drank the water.

Detective Ricosta started to get up, but once again, those little hands with their very tight grip stopped him from doing so. He sat down on the ground next to her once again.

"I...I need to tell you something. In private," she said as she looked at the police and people surrounding them from all sides.

"Sure," he answered as he helped her stand up.

They both went a little deeper into the forest. Once Elizabeth was sure that no one would be able to hear her, she stopped walking. She looked at Detective Ricosta, who was looking at her expectantly.

"I can see the future in my dreams," she started, "That's how I knew that the killer was a woman. That's how I knew that I was soon going to die. I saw it in my dreams. You see, I was born with this strange gift. I'm telling you the truth this time. But you have to believe me. If you don't, my confession will be useless." she said, truth shining in her glassy eyes.

Elizabeth then told him about everything that had happened to her in the past few months. She told him all her dreams.

Detective Alex tried to comprehend her words in his mind. After a few seconds, he finally spoke.

"Okay, I believe you."

And it was believable. Elizabeth couldn't have been in that alley that day. As he thought about her ability, a sudden question invaded his mind.

"You said that you saw the woman. That you've seen her countless times. Then you surely must have seen her face. If you've seen her face, then you can help us find her. Have you seen her face?"

"No, I haven't. I must have, but every time I wake up, her face gets erased from my mind. I don't remember how she looks."

Detective Ricosta sighed. It was all a useless attempt, then.

"Don't worry, Elizabeth; I won't let you die. Now that I know that the killer woman is behind you, I'll try to keep you as safe as possible," he assured her.

"Don't worry about me, Detective. My fate is already decided. Think of yours rather," she said as she left to go back to the graveyard.

It was nighttime. Elizabeth had taken a shower and had even cleared her room of useless stuff. She needed distractions. She brushed her hair while looking in the mirror. Today was surely an unlucky day. After all, she was left to deal with two of her friends' deaths.

She put the brush down and went downstairs into the living room. She looked at her mother's door. It was closed as usual.

Elizabeth walked to the doorframe. She put her fist close to the door, ready to knock. But she stopped midway.

No, it was her secret to keep. She couldn't tell it, anyone. It was wrong. She wouldn't be able to forgive herself if she told the secret she had carefully hidden for so long.

She had a secret hidden among her stars, a deathly secret.

Elizabeth was standing in the far corner of the room in which she was never welcome. It was her mother's room. In the darkness, no one could've noticed her presence.

She looked at her mother, sleeping peacefully. The moonlight from the window cast an angelic look on her face. She looked happy and contented.

Elizabeth smiled at her mother. She took her in with her eyes, each and every feature.

In the business of looking at her mother, she didn't see the shadow that had silently crept inside. It was standing right behind her, its fangs looming over her body.

It came closer, slowly touching Elizabeth's face with its long sharp razor-like fingers. It slowly brought its fingers from her cheek to her jaw. Surprisingly, Elizabeth didn't feel any pain not a drop of blood left her face even though those sharp claws were scratching her face.

Elizabeth was still busy looking at her mother. All of a sudden, Edna's face contorted in pain. She screamed and thrashed in pain. Red liquid started to ooze from her cheeks.

She cried in pain, unable to open her eyes. Elizabeth tried to run toward her mother, but something stopped her.

She turned around to look at the person. A gasp escaped her lips. Before she could've seen its face, it brought its razor-sharp claws to her heart...

Elizabeth stood up from her sleeping position immediately. She was breathing heavily. She looked around her bed for something. Finally, she reached for the glass of water kept on the bedside table.

She picked it up. Her fingers were trembling. She was hiccuping badly. She tried to hold onto the glass, but the glass slipped from her trembling hands.

The water spilled on the bed, splashing everywhere from the blanket to the mattress and finally on Elizabeth's nightgown.

She got off the bed, throwing the blanket on the floor and peeling off the bedsheet from the bed to stop it from soaking in the mattress.

She muttered a string of curses as she looked down at her now completely wet nightgown which was dripping water on the floor.

Picking up the bedsheet and mattress simultaneously, she went to the bathroom to throw them in the laundry bin.

Getting out, she picked up the towel from her closet and once again entered the pink titled bathroom that smelled strongly of roses.

Flicking on the light, she placed the towel on

the hanger. The bathroom looked neat except for the now occupied laundry bin.

Elizabeth went to the sink. Washing her hands with soap, she picked up her toothbrush and started brushing her teeth which smelled like bad cheese to her.

Sliding open the faded white curtain separating the bathtub and the other part of the bathroom, she entered.

The sound of the shower water splashing against the tiled floor was gently followed by silence from the other side.

The cool water seemed to calm Elizabeth down. Her body relaxed as she stood there enjoying the coldness of the liquid, bringing her cells back to life.

After a good ten minutes passed, she closed the shower. She picked up her towel from the glancing metal and draped it across herself.

She reached her hand to slide the curtain away. She felt her hands freeze on their own accord. Condensed away in the air, the smell of fresh cold water was now replaced by the strong scent of iron.

A deep shudder tickled down Elizabeth's spine, making her tremble. She was so busy in her mind that she had not noticed the now red curtain in front of her eyes.

Muffling her scream with her hands, she stared with horror at the curtain; her eyes opened wide. The message was written on the other side, but that didn't stop Elizabeth from understanding it.

She snatched away the curtain with her hands. The metal made a clanking sound as it fell on the cold bathroom floor.

A knock on the door disturbed her before she could do anything. Immediately letting go of the curtain, she went out of the bathroom to open the for to her room.

Standing in front of her was none other than her mother, a frown gracing her pale face.

Elizabeth looked at her mother, waiting for her mother to say something.

"What are you going in there? I just heard a sound. Is something wrong?" she asked.

Pursing her lips into a thin line for a few seconds, she finally let a smile replace it.

"Nothing, mother. I just accidentally stumbled upon something, and the toothbrush holder fell off."

Her voice was confident and completely at ease. Edna nodded slightly as she left for the kitchen.

Elizabeth's bright smile morphed into a deep, dismal frown as she looked at Edna's retreating figure.

Careful not to make a sound, she closed the door silently. She quickly ran to the bathroom, the quiet, melodious shuffle of her feet contrasting with the pink of her room.

She entered the bathroom, her feet a bare whisper against the tiled floor.

She bent down, her long dark hair cascading on her shoulder, following curiously till their tips touched the tiled floor.

She picked up the blood-stained curtain with her fingernails, not wanting to get any of that on her skin.

Deciding to dispose of it later, she threw the curtain in the dustbin. She went where the metal rod had fallen and adjusted it back to its place.

With much effort, the task was finally done. As she stood in front of the basin connected with a mirror, the sound of her hands rubbing together forcefully didn't fail to film the air.

She was trying to get rid of the scent of iron from her fingers. Once done, she sprayed some air freshener to bring the bathroom back to normal.

She slowly closed the bathroom door on her way out. Realizing it was now time for breakfast, she hurriedly picked up a pair of clothes and changed into them.

She left her hair uncombed since she didn't want to deal with her mother's anger at her pointless delay.

Seating herself on the dining table, she came face to face with her mother. A smile settled upon her mother's face as she put down the plates on the table.

Seeing her mother's smile, Elizabeth's own face lit like a bright Christmas tree.

The breakfast went by quietly, with none of them uttering a single word. But it was clear that Edna was having a good day today, which indirectly turned Elizabeth's mood cheerful.

Elizabeth left for school. As she entered high school, she felt a pang in her chest.

No, she needed to focus. She was doing it for a greater cause.

Soon enough, she found Annie. Pairing up together, they both went to their Literature class.

There was not much to tell, nor was there something to listen. It was all a blur, the events that were happening.

The day felt like a roller coaster moving at the speed of an airplane. Elizabeth barely noticed anything interesting as she sucked her pencil deeply, lost in her thoughts.

The day was coming to an end, or at least the school was. As predicted, the loud, high-pitched sound of the bell resonated in the classroom. Students got up from their seats as they hurriedly filed out of their classes, happy that they were now able to go home.

In the way of speaking, the school was pure and utter torture. The studies were sickening, the kids were obnoxious, and the teachers were horrid. Apart from the huge area it covered, there was nothing more endearing than that in the entire school. And so it was nauseating.

Elizabeth slowly got up from her seat, unusually eager to get out of the suffocating building that was spreading its claws delicately on her neck, trying to wait for the right time to strike to choke her to death.

Annie met with her as they got out of the sacred grounds. To be honest, it was the people who called them sacred. To Elizabeth, they looked covered in red whenever she saw them. That's why they were called sacred. It is often the sacred thing that is red.

Love is red; anger is red, and more important than anything, blood is red. And that's exactly what she saw, blood. Blood of her friends and many other innocent girls. If someone were to say from an outsider's point, her own crimson red stained the area.

Annie left Elizabeth's home as Elizabeth kept toying around with the seatbelt all the way home, long lost in her own poisonous thoughts.

Elizabeth walked the steep pavement as she walked to her house. She bent down, her long hair cascading down her face as she picked up the key hidden beneath the plant pot, which smelled freshly of mud and roses.

Unlocking the door, her hand touched the doorknob with her lean but little fingers when she heard it. The utter desolate and gut-wrenching silence from the other side. The idea of opening the door itself felt unwelcoming.

Deep down, she knew something was utterly wrong when she touched the doorknob and felt the cold metal harassing her skin.

The silence was daring, completely unusual. It was never this silent in the house. Her mother was always doing something, whether it be cooking or chatting with Celeste, her mother's best friend who often visited the house.

Elizabeth wondered why Celeste had not come to meet her mother for a month. It was unusual for her not to visit, but it was plainly Celeste's choice.

Suddenly out of nowhere, the thick yet fragile glass of silence shattered into pieces as she heard a loud thud as if something had fallen on the ground.

Elizabeth turned the doorknob. Opening the door wide, she was met by the sudden blow of wind coming from the open windows of the other side of the house. Her hair covered her vision. She turned them behind and looked at the scenario laid in front of her.

She nearly collapsed as she looked at the two persons sitting on the red floor in front of her, the bright light from outside illuminating their faces.

She ran towards the twitching body that was lying on the crimson floor. Fresh blood was oozing out from the big hole in the person's stomach where the knife had assaulted her body.

Her eyes then moved toward the person sitting against her, a person she would never be able to call her own. She averted her eyes from the person as a wave of hate passed through her body, screaming for revenge.

A pool of blood was starting to form around the half-dead body of the woman that lay there on the cold dead floor, the warmth of the woman's blood emanating from the frostbitten floor.

Elizabeth slowly, with shaking fingers, touched those twitching fingers of the woman as she herself tried to stop the escaping tears from her betraying eyes. Elizabeth's whole body was trembling, the sound of her labored breaths sounder than the gushing wind that flew in through the open windows.

Her uncontrollable tears turned into sobs, resonating through the room. Short and suffocated, her breath was as she held those hands that were losing their warmth.

"Mother," she whispered, her voice cracking in between. "Stay awake."

Her mother let out a tired sigh. Her lips held

together a second ago with the strong pull of her teeth were now released and spilling blood. The knife in her stomach was more prominent than ever.

"It is time for me to leave," she barely managed to speak as she coughed some blood on the already crimson floor.

"No, mother. Please don't go. I'm begging you. Stay awake. I'm going to call the ambulance. Just don't close your eyes."

Before Elizabeth could stand up, she felt soft fingers wrap around her hand, holding her back from leaving.

"No. I'm afraid I don't have much time. So let me tell you something."

"No, mother, no, " Elizabeth said, crying.

"Elizabeth, my dear, all I was trying to do was to protect you from the monster that your father is, but I didn't realize that between protecting you from him, I had become one too...I love you; at least you know now that your mother wasn't always a monster.",

Edna said as her eyes started losing light.

"Please don't go. Mother, please don't leave me."

"I'm glad that I now have no guilt. Let me go, my dear."

With that, Edna's eyes fluttered closed, never to be opened once again.

With bloodshot eyes, she looked up at the man sitting in front of her. A flame was dancing in her eyes, ready to burn down the man who had killed her mother.

Clearly, Maxin Montgomery was not and will never be her father. A father is a person who cares about both his wife and child. In Elizabeth's eyes, Maxin Montgomery had failed the test.

"Elizabeth, my love, let me explain. I didn't want to do this. Your mother forced me. She denied me to have you back. I tried, I honestly did. But your mother was so stubborn; she pushed me out.

You know, the only thing I ever wanted was a child to take care of. Your mother did wrong, and she knew it. Maybe this was her punishment. She is gone now and can't be brought back. Come with me, your father. Elizabeth, please come with me. I promise I won't ever hurt you."

He extended an arm towards Elizabeth, wishing for her to hold it.

Elizabeth nodded in denial, her eyes still watery. Maxon's features turned angry in a matter of seconds as he stared at Elizabeth's rheumy blue eyes.

Letting out a deep, irritated sigh, he launched himself at Elizabeth. Elizabeth shrieked loudly as he put his steely grip on her left hand, his nails digging into her soft red flesh. Her voice was hoarse, so the scream felt like nothing but a bare whisper in the chilly wind that draped their town in a curtain of heavenly beauty.

He dragged her towards the open window, possibly planning to escape from there. Elizabeth screamed louder, her voice sounding a bit more prominent this time.

Before Maxon's hand could reach her mouth to

silence her, his whole body retracted wildly as the small metal body passed through his back, penetrating deep within till it touched his chest.

His grip loosened on Elizabeth's arm as he fell to the ground. Yet another pool of blood was starting to form in the room.

Elizabeth turned around to look at the person who fired the gun. Being drained of any energy left inside her body, her movements were slow.

Standing a few feet away was none other than the Detective, whom she failed to understand completely. Elizabeth's vision was turning blurry by the second. She saw the Detective run towards her. She felt those hands grabbing her and making her sit on the sofa. The touch was gone, but she soon felt it again as those hands made her drink water.

"Elizabeth, stay awake. I'm calling the team and the ambulance. Just don't close your eyes," said Detective Mary as she held Elizabeth with one hand and the phone in the other.

In a matter of seconds, the place was a blur of onergy. Aura, that's what she had learned. The auras of humans never died, so maybe her mom's aura was there somewhere, mixed with a hundred others that were occupying the house at that very moment.

Her eyes were closing, not due to weakness or hunger. She was far behind human desires and pain. She wanted to close her eyes, for she needed to think. She needed to think that her mother was here, and she needed not to look at the people filing in.

Before her eyes could've closed, Detective Ricosta touched her cheeks. She looked at him, the pain still visible in her eyes.

"I'm sorry about your mother. It's not okay, I know. Everything will not be okay, but at least everything is not pure chaos. The department believes that Maxon Montgomery was behind the murder. They are closing the case now. You don't have to worry now. You're safe."

With that, he left as the forensics team called him.

Annie soon arrived. She came running through the door, going straight towards Elizabeth. She held Elizabeth in a hug as Elizabeth cried against her clothes.

She kept patting Elizabeth, hoping for her to get okay, hoping to see her normal once again. But then again, it wasn't her decision to make. It was Elizabeth's.

She mourned to herself as she looked at Elizabeth's desolate collapsing psyche. She didn't know what was going to happen now, but one thing she did know.

Elizabeth was going to fall.

Annie rushed Elizabeth out of the Victorian house as the neighbors and many other people started filing in to witness the murder and sympathize with a shaking, petrified and blood-covered Elizabeth.

She hurriedly took the poor, shocked, befuddled, and thoroughly heartbroken girl to her car, carefully tucking her inside in the passenger seat and securing the seatbelt tightly over her petite frame.

Shutting the door that made a clicking sound, she went to the other side of the car, got inside, and fastened the seatbelt to her body.

With one push to the accelerator, the car roared to life, its engine snorting loudly like a dragon clashing its tail as Annie dashed the car out of the neighborhood.

Elizabeth's body was still shaking violently as she tried her hardest to control the tears pricking at her eyes. Annie let her hand brush off Elizabeth's long golden hair to create a feeling of comfort, holding Elizabeth's hand in her own, trying to calm her friend.

She herself tried to control the upcoming tears. No matter how much she hated Aunt Edna, she was a crucial part of Elizabeth's life, and now that she was gone, Annie was afraid that Elizabeth would collapse.

Annie was driving straight, taking a few turns here and there, wanting to get to her home as soon as possible. There she would be finally able to nurse and comfort Elizabeth.

The sun was peacefully setting over the horizon, its scarce rays giving the surroundings a deep shade of hue and dust. The meagerly sparse rays soon disappeared somewhere in infinity as darkness began its rule.

Elizabeth was still shaking violently, though her sobs were now barely perceptible. She sat on the car seat like a wall as she stared into space, the numbness within her deepening with each passing minute.

Darkened was her heart now, with the wickedness that was slowly starting to latch itself onto the pages of the book of her life.

With her unblinking eyes and face as cold as the frost that was slowly moving towards their town, anyone could have mistaken her for a dead body.

Annie's car moved smoothly across the concrete floor, with the muffled sounds of small rocks and pebbles crushing under the tires' weight.

The darkness masterly combined with the black-grey roads as the eerie yet calm silence hung in the hollow air inside the claustrophobic walls of the car.

A scream of horror was perceived in Elizabeth's ears as the car skewered right. She was brutally jerked towards the passenger door. The loud, clangor thudding of her head against the window was one of the dumbest yet painstakingly horrible sounds she had ever heard, next to her mother's last words to her.

Slowly enough, she slightly moved her head away from the door.

Her hand moved to the corner of her forehead where blood spilled from the burning gash cast darkly on her ghastly pale and brittle face. Her eyes wandered everywhere by themselves, unable to focus on anything as she spun momentarily like a pendulum.

Blurred and mirrored images of things nonsensical to her brain passed through her sight. The fog shed upon her vision slowly dispersed as the mirrored images marring her view no longer appeared.

She saw a body lying unconscious next to her from her blurred peripheral vision.

Annie.

Hastened, she untied her seatbelt.

The door made a creaking noise as Elizabeth weakly scurried out of the passenger seat. She almost unlocked Annie's belt with feeble hands, dragging her out from the passenger seat.

Annie's warm face was stained with sweat, and a few cuts and scratches scattered over her face.

The car beside them looked desolate and broken. The front metal was now scraped out; the vibrant colors now peeled off from the edges. It looked just as smashed as a crumpled ball of paper due to its harsh impact as it came crashing down the huge brick wall.

The wall looked unaffected, though, wearing a proud smile of victory as it held its ground. With its chest put forward in a manner of appalling boldness, the wall boasted silently of its strength and brutality.

The air was now thinner than a sheet of aluminum, the shades of gloominess and obscurity lurking beyond the veils of countless errors bundled up together in the crepuscular alley.

The two desperate, helpless, disheartened girls sitting on the dirty floor looked indistinct and vaguely detectable in the pitch-black darkness surrounding the foreboding, musty place.

Elizabeth, with frantic movements, tried to bring a peaceful Annie back to the mortal state of senses and pain, to the world of momentary gains and losses by tapping lightly on her chin again and again.

Annie slowly stirred in Elizabeth's embrace, a soft moan coming from her mouth. Twitching her eyebrows forcefully, she slowly tried to open her drunken eyes.

As Elizabeth gashed face came into her blue vision, she wriggled out of Elizabeth's grasp, frantically forcing herself to sit.

She opened her mouth slightly but closed it again, unable to form coherent words. A mixture of sweat and tears covered her face as she stared at Elizabeth with wide, broken eyes.

"I... I am so... sorry, Liz," she apologized, choking on her words.

Elizabeth opened her mouth to speak but was cut off by Annie's preposterous words.

"I... The car... it hit something... I tried... I tried to control... but it won't stop... the wall... I'm so sorry..."

Before she could've muttered another word, Elizabeth's fingers moved to Annie's lips. She felt Elizabeth's warm hug, followed by muffled sobs of her own.

"How will we... reach home now? I... I don't even have my phone... I left it when... I was at your... home. Do you... have your... phone, Liz?" She asked countless questions as she continued to sob against Liz's shoulder.

"No, I don't have my phone. Don't worry, Ann, we will be okay. You see that warehouse?" Elizabeth said, pointing towards an abandoned warehouse, "We are going to stay there tonight. We will figure out what to do in the morning."

Elizabeth stood up; dusting the dirt particles from her clothes, she reached her hand towards Annie.

With shaking fingers, Annie took Liz's hand and got up. Her feet were jelly. Barely able to stand, she grabbed Elizabeth's arm for support.

The soft sounds of their feet were heard moving towards the old, abandoned warehouse.

The warehouse didn't look appealing, with its distasteful brown color. The roof was uneven, and some bricks were missing atop. From a stranger's eyes, it would've made the perfect setting for a horror movie.

A loud creak welcomed them as Elizabeth fumbled with the lock. The warm scent of coffee assaulted their desperate souls, meeting them inside.

Annie weakly wobbled inside. Elizabeth watched carefully as Annie made her way inside. She fished out the phone from her pockets while keeping a strict eye on Annie.

A bright light came across her eyes as she tapped the screen. She typed a message and placed the phone in her pocket again.

She silently ran towards Annie so that they were close to each other. Annie's black hair bounced slightly as she turned towards Elizabeth.

A weak smile broke out on Annie's lips as she drank in Elizabeth's familiar features.

"God! Something is absolutely wrong with me. I'm becoming way too paranoid these days," she said in a whispered tone.

"What's wrong?" Elizabeth asked.

"Nothing. I just thought that you weren't behind me. See, I am overthinking things."

"Don't worry; I'll always be there for you, I promise."

They were distracted as another wave of warmness hit their worn souls.

Elizabeth walked towards the source of the heavenly smell, with Annie following behind. They had reached a kitchen-like room.

Elizabeth let her hands roam against the wall. Her hands finally reached a tiny pull handle. She let it pushed it in upwards direction.

Dim light flooded the room as the orange bulb hanging from the ceiling flickered, opening and closing vigorously. The illuminating orange rays hit the wall, making them appear like walls of flames dancing at midnight.

The reflection was thrown on the black counters where the coffee maker sat patiently, waiting for someone to make some use out of it.

[Annie limped her way towards the door attached beside the counter. She let it open as she entered the huge mast of darkness. As she placed her hand on the wall for support, her hand found the light switch. She let the switch slide up.

Bright flicking light filled the cramped space inside the room as the bulb glowed in a bright shade of fiery orange.

Scattered files brilliantly sat on the old metal table filled with a hundred drawers containing files, papers sticking out of the surface placed in between. Two chairs were sitting near it, facing each other. The wall behind it was covered with pictures of various murder cases that had been taken in town, a web of threads branching them together.

Annie's mouth was wide open as she stared at the newly added pictures of the mutilated girls across the city.

Holding the two clean and warm coffee mugs in her hand, Elizabeth's feet carried her towards the door. Her face transformed into a mixture of confusion and distaste as she looked at Annie's back, blocking her way.

Her body went rigid when she noticed the reason for Annie's sudden shift in behavior. A cold shiver ran down her spine as she stared at the disgusting webbed pictures.

Beads of sweat started to form around her hands. The mugs clashed with the floor as they slipped out of her fingers, spilling the boiling liquid on Annie's legs.

Annie fell down on the floor from the burning sensation. A painful moan escaped her lips as she held the back of her thighs.

Elizabeth hurriedly crouched down and helped Annie to stand up. She made Annie sit on the chair she had barely managed to pull out with her free hand.

A loud cry escaped Annie's plump lips as she held onto her legs.

Elizabeth tried to nurse Annie as she tore the lining of Annie's jeans from the knees.

"Ann, I'm so sorry. I..."

"It's okay. Umm... Liz... is there a washroom

here? Could we search for it, please?" she pleaded, holding her face in pain.

"Okay. Let's go. Can you walk, or do you need me to hold you?"

"No, I will walk myself."

Annie placed her petite hand on the back of the chair as she stood on her legs. The burning sensation had now ceased, but the hot searing pain in her burned red flesh was still there.

Both of them walked through the kitchen. The pitch darkness greeted their vision as soon as they left the dimly lit kitchen.

After a few minutes of countless feeble walking, they reached a doorknob. Elizabeth turned it around and entered the room with Annie limping beside her.

Elizabeth felt squishy liquid run down her bare arm, sending cold shivers down her warm skin. She shuddered as her eyes slowly moved upwards. This time, she felt the liquid fall on her forehead and then her hand.

She brought her hand closer to her nose. The strong scent of iron nipped at her senses. A gag escaped her lips as she tried to wipe off the droplets from her hand and face.

Annie started at Elizabeth, who had been moving her hands absentmindedly in the air for a long time, confused at her strange behavior.

She soon felt something squishy on her face. She looked upwards at where the liquid was dripping from.

The floorboards above them whispered and creaked as more of that squishy, slippery, and distasteful substance fell through the holes and empty spaces on the roof. The creaking grew louder as the pieces of wood snapped, the liquid falling on the girls getting thicker.

A loud snap reverberated in the air as the roof came crashing down in front of the girls. Their screams

mixed with the devastation as they backed away. Annie ran back as far as possible, screaming.

Her back touched with something solid and pointy. She screamed more loudly as the old pointy thing harassed her from behind.

The dim light bulb suddenly came to life, flickering with the burning ambers growing proudly inside it.

A synchronized scream of pain and horror came from the girls' mouth as their hands flew to their mouths.

Elizabeth gulped, tears coming from her eyes as she saw the devastating view laid in front of her eyes.

There, in a pool of blood and vomit, was a stale body of a girl. The body had a knife passed through her heart.

Elizabeth turned around to run out, her hair falling on her sweaty, bloody face. A cry escaped her lips as she felt the cold blade pierce through her right ear. Blood spewed from the wound inflicted on her from nowhere.

Her own blood.

A moan came from her lips as her knees buckled down; with a soft thud, she collapsed on the slippery, wet, damp, and dismal ground.

Annie rushed towards Elizabeth, covered in a distasteful shade of crimson from head to toe. She distracted her eyes from the body whose blood was now spilled over both her and Liz.

She held a shaking Liz in her hands; her own body trembled along with Liz. Tears escaped her own eyes as she saw Liz moan and thrash in her embrace, the knife still stuck in Liz's ear.

"Liz..." She whispered, her voice barely reaching her own ears.

"Liz," She said more firmly this time, "I...I am going.. to be taking this knife out... If I don't... remove it, you'll... catch an infection. Stay still... please."

Her voice croaked as she looked at Liz's face, filled with an ugly mixture of blood and sweat. Dry blood stuck to her blonde hair.

Annie knew that Elizabeth's state perfectly reflected her own.

Liz silently blinked her eyes, too afraid to open her mouth as she struggled with words to find to describe her pain.

"It... it hurts," she mumbled as more tears flowed out from her eyes. She wiped her nose with her bloody hands and sobbed.

She winced, her mouth partly opened, creases decorating her forehead as she felt Annie's hand slide to the freezing metal.

With one gentle squeeze, Annie pulled the knife out in a quick move. Elizabeth flinched and let out a cry.

She kept crying as more blood spilled from her ear. Her sobs died as a few minutes passed in

Annie's warm, red embrace.

Annie choked and gulped as she saw Elizabeth quiet down. The blood from Liz's ear was a waterfall on its own, not expecting to stop at any moment.

She needed to do something before it was too late.

"Liz I am going to bring the first aid kit from the car. Wait here...and don't... I repeat...don't close your eyes no matter what happens."

Annie got up from the floor as unfolded her legs. The ground seemed to stir as she drunkenly made her exit through the door.

Elizabeth perceived the sound of the door closing with a soft bang.

Ann left her alone.

Elizabeth sat silently surrounded by a pool liquid of crimson, her clothes splattered and stained by her blood, her blonde hair soaked with a mixture of dried crimson red as she remembered the knife that appeared so quickly from within the darkness filling her with terror from within the washroom, which was only dimly lit from the kitchen and the dampness of water droplets thick with the smell of iron.

From the sharp pain of a knife piercing her right ear, to the warmish, hot blood spilling endlessly to what appeared never-ending. Then lying on the cold floor was the sight of a girl's body decapitated. It all seemed like a nightmare. Maybe if she only closed her eyes, it all would disappear, and she could finally wake up from this hellish nightmare and find herself home, knowing it was nothing but a bad dream.

Her eyes slowly started losing sight as her blinking pace slowed down.

Her eyes flew open as Annie's loud shriek started to echo down the warehouse. Annie burst into the room as her face came into view.

Even though Annie's whole face was covered, Elizabeth didn't fail to notice the gash running through Annie's cheeks.

"Liz..run..she..she..is here," She said, out of breath

Annie's knees buckled down as they started losing weight, and her bones started crushing under each other as she slowly collapsed on the floor.

Elizabeth's eyes widened, a sweat trickle ran down her forehead, her hair now dried and tickling with blood. She got up at a rushed pace on wobbly feet, falling once again on her knees.

She dragged herself out of the room with the help of four limbs. As she burst out of the door, she slowly got on her feet, running outside, her feet making weird noises as they tapped on the floorboards.

Elizabeth put a hand on her head, covering the huge dent in her head, where fresh blood was gushing through her hair, making them damp again.

Crimson coated her vision as the blood stuck at her long lashes, contrasting with the black in them.

Elizabeth's eyes eventually closed on their own; as she stirred momentarily. Dark red covered her vision, and with a hand placed on her head, she collapsed to the side.

Her eyes started to open slowly, her eyebrows creased, a premature swell set on her angelic red face Her eyes started to open slowly, her eyebrows creased, a premature swell set on her angelic red face.

All the blood had dried up, her dry hair sticking out of her face and ground, her clothes stuck tightly to her body like bodycon.

The surroundings turned into one scenic void, the colors of the darkness and deceit micing together to make a peaceful tapestry of screams and pain that was scaring to squeeze out of her pulsated veins as she blinked her eyes rapidly.

The obscure spots around her perception cleared away as she slowly dangled up from the dark flooring. With a hand put on her head and the other on the passageway of the foreboding alley, she pulled herself to sit.

Her eyes zoomed in as they focused on the hazy figure with long dark hair blowing back and forth as the soft wind buzzed down the alley.

Her own breath hitched when she felt the wind gently tickling her neck, sending a quiver through her body.

"Our little princess is finally awake," a womanly voice blooms while cackling loudly.

A voice she had recognized well enough forever.

"Wh...why?" she cracks, a fresh tear escaping the dark circled pieces of her sight.

The woman stifled a laugh at the silly question of her destined victim.

"You know why," The lady whispered in a low voice, her hair falling in front of her, covering her face as she lowered her face towards Elizabeth. The gash was still prominent on her evil face.

"All my life, I've been told how unworthy and useless I am, how I am nothing compared to you, or Marina, or June. You're more beautiful than me, Marina was kinder than me, and June was smarter than me. I've been compared with almost every girl in the town, and you know what, Liz? It doesn't feel good at all."

Annie says as she looks at Elizabeth with a wicked grin plastered on her face.

"I...how...did?"

"How did I manage to do all this? You see, Liz, it was all very easy, too easy if you ask me. You had given me a spare key to your house two years ago, so entering and leaving your house on my will wasn't a problem at all.

"As for the others, yes, I killed them. I killed them all because they were better than me, much better. Don't worry though, I'll make your death very special since you're my best friend.

"This time, even that detective friend of yours won't be able to save you because he is too busy pulling off the case close and grieving over poor Aunt Edna." Elizabeth stared at Annie with petrified blue eyes. She opened her mouth but closed it once again.

"I...did you kill my mother?" she asked, hate gleaming in her crystal eyes as she stared at the traitor, anger set on her red lips.

Annie sighed as she intently dozed off while

staring at the foggy atmosphere, the wind playing with her long dark hair.

"I never wanted Aunt Edna to die. I didn't even know you had a father, but I am kind of glad he killed Aunt Edna. It made my plan much easier."

Tears dotted Elizabeth's wide round eyes. She blinked rapidly as the tears threatened to spill from the ravaged action of misery and hurt.

She took in a deep breath, the tears lurking in the shadows of those dark droopy bags surrounding her eyes.

She let her eyelids blink back to darkness, her lips curled upwards, despite the lump building in her scratchy throat.

Annie moved her hand to her jean's back pocket and pulled out the strange metal that had been resting there. She held it as if it were light fur.

The metal gleamed in the dark as Annie moved forward towards Elizabeth, her footsteps reverberating in the alley.

Bending down towards the ground, her fierce eyes met Elizabeth's dark closed ones.

"You asked me once to complete your story without realizing that you gave me permission to end it myself. This is the end, Liz, the end that you wanted, the end you craved for," she whispered in Elizabeth's ears, her long hair brushing Elizabeth's cheeks.

Annie's grip on the gleaming, polished metal tightened. She traveled it lightly over Elizabeth's legs, careful not to hurt her.

The knife moved across Elizabeth's bare arms, tilting towards her chest.

Annie's knuckles turned white as she let out a shaky smile.

The knife plunged into Elizabeth's heavily breathing chest. Her breathing ceased as her lips parted slightly, her eyes wide open.

Blood gushed out from the gleaming weapon, inking Annie's hand Elizabeth's blood.

The watery feeling tickled her legs as she felt the blood spreading further on her legs. The warmth returned to her body as the crimson liquid splashed on her face.

Annie jerked away from the knife, a tear escaping her eyes. Shaking violently, she got onto her feet and looked at Elizabeth's disheveled-haired wide-eyed, terrified corpse lying on the floor.

She had killed Liz. It was her fault.

She gulped the bile rising in her throat.

She had won.

Annie's hair hit her face as she turned around. Her feet paddocked the asphalt as she frantically tried to distance herself from Liz.

The loud screeching metal echoed in the air as Annie's legs were forced to stop, her feet unmoving and rigid. Quivering like a sick person left out in the cold, her chapped lips opened, and her lashes fluttered down to her stomach. Blood came out from the small hole in her stomach where the small bullet had just pierced her skin.

She felt it all. The way her tissues contracted as they tore apart, the bundle of the nerves breaking away as the bullet twisted and turned inside her skin. Her organs betrayed her as they paused their work. Her heart slowly died, her chest rising and falling, the motion getting slower each second.

Her hands touched her belly, trying to lighten the pain of the metal ripping at her flesh.

Her knees gave away as she collapsed on the floor, her blood-stained hands were set at weird angles, and blood spilled from her stomach where the cold metal had destroyed the flesh.

In the far corner of the alley, Detective Ricosta was standing, the gun sticking out of his hands.

He had seen that dark figurine fall on the ground after he had fired the shot. It was so dark that he was barely able to make out the girl's face except for her long dark hair.

It was not Elizabeth.

He knew something was wrong when he got her strange text saying goodbye.

Detective Mary was standing by his side, trying to tell him something, but he was too busy searching for Elizabeth to listen to her words.

He ran towards the girl he had just shot. He switched on the flashlight of his phone. A surprised expression marked his face as he saw himself standing next to none other than Annie herself.

The sweet girl Elizabeth had befriended.

"Alex!" bellowed Detective Mary in horror.

He looked around in the dark. Squinting his eyes, he noticed Mary standing farther away, holding her own mobile, its light flashing violently on him.

He ran towards her; Detective Mary diverted the flashlight to the ground. A gasp escaped his lips as he stared at the seventeen-year-old girl whose wide blue eyes and golden hair didn't fail to make his heart beat faster.

She still looked so beautiful.

Detective Mary called the whole team to come as soon as possible while Detective Alex was unable to do anything but stare at the innocent girl.

He remembered her words at the meadow.

"Don't worry about me, detective. My fate is already decided. Think of yours rather," She had said in her honey-like voice.

How could she not know that he had already chosen her as his fate?

He closed his eyes as he zoned out, trying to deafen the sound of heavy footsteps and police sirens.

He closed his eyes as he zoned out, trying to deafen the sound of heavy footsteps and police sirens. Alex rummaged through his chest, trying to find something to wear. He picked up a white shirt. The sound of something light weighted as it fell on the floor was almost negligible as the enveloped paper fell on his toes.

He looked down at the enveloped letter.

Elizabeth's letter.

A sense of nostalgia and regret filled his mind as he bent down to pick up the letter.

Elizabeth had asked him not to open the letter until she told him to, but now that she was gone, nothing was holding him back from opening it.

He took out the folded piece of paper from the torn envelope attached to another piece of paper. With much creasing of his eyebrows, he slowly unfolded the paper.

His gaze went to the inked words written in an overly graceful manner. He read the letter repeatedly, unable to believe his eyes.

He gripped the frame of his bed. Crumpled was now the paper as he threw it on the floor.

Elizabeth did not just unravel a secret among those pages; she had managed to write a truth hidden amongst the mist he had failed to disown in the case he wanted so badly to solve.

Elizabeth did not just unravel a secret among those pages; she had managed to write a truth hidden amongst the mist he had failed to disown in the case he wanted so badly to solve

A dustbin lay in the far corner of Elizabeth's tiled bathroom. There, inside the dustbin, laid a curtain, its blood-bold red letters shining inside the thin black sheet.

Dreams are not what you say they are.

Black spots dotted the fairly cold, shivering grounds. There was no downpour this time; no weeping sound admits the people. There were no ghosts of past or present regretting over the cruel happenings of the painful past.

No mourn, no loss, nor guilt was pitied upon Annie. Though, the loss was expressed for Edna and Elizabeth.

As Alex looked at the brooding, unforgiving mass of people, his heart went out to Elizabeth's words.

Her last few words for him, only him.

He went towards the podium set up for the Mayor. Tapping his fingers slightly on the mic, all the heads snapped toward his direction.

The people stared at him in confusion, their mouths partly open, their eyes bloodshot.

Alex sighed deeply before pulling his face closer to the mic, "I have something important to tell you."

Frowns were greeted by this as there were whispers. People readied themselves to hear what the Detective had to say.

"As you all know, we've come here today to mark our presence at the funeral of Elizabeth Scottson, Edna Scottson, and Annie Bradshaw. I think that by now, each of you knows what happened, but I'm sure that I'll be able to prove your belief wrong.

"I'm afraid the townspeople have been kept away from the knowledge of the actual series of events, and I think that it's time that you know the truth.

"Elizabeth Scottson was a liar, a great actress, and even a better manipulator. Elizabeth lied to the police; she was unable to see the future in her dreams. She made up those stories, and she made them well enough too.

"That ability of hers brings me to a question. What tempted her to lie? What must have gone wrong with a seventeen-year-old girl who forced her to do all this?

"Elizabeth suffered from anxiety and constant depression. She was a broken girl who carried the weight of her broken wings on her shoulders and yet managed to stand. All she failed was to walk with them.

"Elizabeth was not given the importance or love

she should have given in her childhood. This had a deafening impact on her. This turned her into a liar. She was just yet another casualty of the fire of tyranny of brutal perception.

"She was scorned. Her mind didn't work the way it should have; all she ever learned was the art of weaving a tapestry of lies. She kept us all in the dark till her death.

"Elizabeth knew her best friend was a killer but kept it a secret.

"But we can't blame Elizabeth for that, nor can we blame Edna for not loving her daughter because that would be a major lie. Edna loved her daughter way more than anything; all she was trying to do was protect her daughter.

"As for Mr. Montgomery, I can't find it in myself to blame him either. All he wanted was his daughter. We can't possibly blame a man for loving his child to the furthest limits.

"In the much bigger picture comes Annie Bradshaw.

"She was kind of complex. Annie Bradshaw was sometimes the sweet, simple, and cheerful girl. While sometimes, she was a ruthless, cold-hearted lady who didn't care about who she killed.

"She must've not killed these girls without a cause. There must have been a rational reason for what she did. I wondered about this, too, but Elizabeth's final letter to me cleared all my doubts.

"Annie had multiple personality disorder, plain and simple. Her father always used to make her feel down by constantly comparing her to everyone since childhood. And for a small child, this was impossible to deal with alone.

"Annie kept it all trapped in her heart until one day; one became her own poison. It was inflicted on her mind that many were better than her, and whoever was better needed to be erased from existence.

"Annie's mind worked in a way even she was not able to comprehend. We can't blame her; how can we call her evil? She was just a sweet, simple girl who wanted nothing but love.

"Elizabeth and Edna Scottson were victims, and so were Mr. Montgomery and Annie.

"I came here not to speak in their funeral but to deliver a message that I wish you all engrave in your memory forever, for if you don't, I'm afraid death and pain will come on swift showers of misery and illness upon the town like a plague once again.

"Without further ado, I will deliver the message I was asked to deliver. A question.

"If these people are not to blame, then who is?

"The answer to this question was very difficult, but like always, Elizabeth didn't fail to answer it simply.

"Society is the one to blame. We are the ones to blame

"Elizabeth turned into a liar because of the ignorance she suffered from. Edna turned into a cold person because of the thorns she had in her life. Maxon turned into a killer because he was declined of the simplest thing in his life, his daughter. Annie turned into a monster because of the constant forms she faced.

"I want you all to think about this and remember my words before saying anything to anyone, even if it's your children."

He gulped audibly as his grip loosened from the mic. A deep silence met his words.

No whispers.

Alex looked at the people, a thin line marking his face. He walked down the podium, his feet paddocking the ground as he moved towards the three dark caskets placed on the ground.

He looked at the sleeping Elizabeth, a sigh escaping his lips. Bending down and taking out the gift from his pocket, he placed the white rose in her cold hands before he closed the casket.

A white flower for the kindest girl.

He had done what she had asked for. He had fulfilled her last wish. He hoped that her soul now be able to rest in peace.

The End

OTHER BOOKS BY THE AUTHOR

Karmic Love

Undercover

Eternal Love

Undying Lust

The Good Taste

Offence and Justice

A Model for Murder

Lethal Legacy

Lethal Legacy 2

Paranormal Club

Enchanted Souls

Beginners of Nowhere

Wildflower

Mystic Agent

Dark Angel

Lonesome Moonlight

The Eerie Egg

A Romantic Crime .

Passionate Alien

Dragon Knight

The Critical Case

In the Shadow

Mental Asylum

Athena

Candy Spy